For Vanessa, my splendid collaborator ~ J.H.

For Mum ~ T.F.

First published 2006 by Walker Books Ltd, 87 Vauxhall Walk, London SE11 5HJ 10 9 8 7 6 5 4 3 2 1
Text ©2006 Judy Hindley. Illustrations ©2006 Tor Freeman. The right of Judy Hindley and Tor Freeman to be identified as author and illustrator respectively of this work has been asserted by them in accordance with the Copyright, Designs and Patents Act 1988. This book has been typeset in Lemonade. Printed in China. All rights reserved. No part of this book may be reproduced, transmitted or stored in an information retrieval system in any form or by any means, graphic, electronic or mechanical, including photocopying, taping and recording, without prior written permission from the publisher. British Library Cataloguing in Publication Data: a catalogue record for this book is available from the British Library ISBN-13: 978-0-7445-9651-9 ISBN-10: 0-7445-9651-3 www.walkerbooks.co.uk

Sleepy Places

Kiss
Kiss!

Judy Hindley

illustrated by

Tor Freeman

WALKER BOOKS
AND SUBSIDIARIES
LONDON • BOSTON • SYDNEY • AUCKLAND

When you're yawning and nodding and flopping,
and ready to fall in a heap,
where do you choose for a nap or a snooze
– where is your favourite place to sleep?

A rabbit sleeps tight in its burrow;

a bird snuggles down in a tree.

SNORE

A frog takes
a snooze in
the ooze of a pond;

a rose makes
a bed for a bee.

Do you suppose you could drowse in a rose,

or snooze in the ooze

like a frog?

A cat can nap on
somebody's hat;
a bear curls up
in a cave.

A fish may dream in
the reeds of a stream;

a seal lolls about
on a wave...

Can you imagine what dreams you'd have,

lolling about on a wave?

A swift can sleep
on the wing as it flies;

a horse
can sleep on
the hoof;

bats hang
upside
down from
their toes,
in rows
upon rows
in the roof.

If you were a bat,
you'd sleep like that,
upside down
in the roof!

A pup likes to sleep

in a quivering heap,

with a bundle of sisters and brothers.

Kangaroo joeys
tuck themselves
up in pockets
attached
to their
mothers.

But what about you?

What place do you choose

– what sleepy place

for a nap

or a snooze?

A nest of cushions,

a cave of quilts,

a bundle of pillows ...

a cot,

a pram?

A hammock,

a sofa,

a box,

a rug,

a comfy lap,

a cuddly arm?

Or would you choose your own little bed,
with your own little blanket and pillow,

and kisses and stories and teddies and things,
and somebody tucking you in?

Oh yes -
we each have a
favourite sleepy place...

Goodnight!